P9-BBO-885

Roaming Riley

A Delmarva Adventure

Allison Wiest

ISBN 978-1-62806-286-1 (print | paperback)

Library of Congress Control Number 2020910215

Published by Salt Water Media
29 Broad Street, Suite 104
Berlin, MD 21811
www.saltwatermedia.com

Cover art and illustrations by Tracey Arvidson
Chapter title illustrations by Madelyn Wiest

Visit the author's website: www.allisonwiest.com

Dedication

For Kevin, who simply said,
"What if you stay home and write?"

Chapter 1
A Cozy Spot

"Where are you going this time, Daddy?" Rosie is sitting on the bed watching her dad pack for another business trip. I stretch out alongside her and purr while she scratches my head.

"This one's close, sweetheart," he replies, putting another shirt on top of the pile in his suitcase. "It's just across the bridge in Ocean City. Want me to bring you back a treat from Candy Kitchen?"

"One of the big lollipops! Those are my favorite," answers Nicki, Rosie's younger sister, who just walked into the room. She crumples up a paper ball, shakes it around a little, and then throws it. I dart into action, just as she knew I would.

"Bring it back, Riley!" she yells down the hallway. I walk slowly back with the ball in my mouth and drop it at her feet, quietly begging her to toss it again. Of course she does. I can always count on Nicki to play with me.

"I like peanut butter fudge the best," says Rosie, "and Mom loves anything salted caramel. You should bring her a surprise too."

"One big lollipop, peanut butter fudge, and salted caramel. Got it. Maybe I'll pick up some Fishers popcorn on my way out of town too," says Dad, as he packs the last of his things. "Let's go say goodbye to Mom, and then I'll come back and grab my suitcase."

I watch as the kids leave the room with their dad. Sadly, I drop the paper ball onto the ground, batting it around a few times with my paw since nobody is here to throw it for me anymore. That's when I notice Dad's open suitcase. All of the warm, cozy clothing looks like it is just waiting for me to snuggle up in it. I climb on top and dig my way down into the clothes until I find the perfect spot to sleep. Nestled up between a soft Orioles sweatshirt and Dad's Ravens pajama pants, I close my eyes and settle in for a catnap.

Chapter 2
Road Trip

"Davis gets up to bat. He's 1 for 3 tonight and hoping he can turn it around for the Birds. He gets set at the plate. It's a fastball to the inside corner..."

I wake up to hear snippets from the Orioles game and assume one of the girls turned on the TV. I blink slowly and notice that it's really dark. That's odd. It's summertime and shouldn't be this dark already. As I move my head around, it brushes up against some socks, and I realize I'm still in Dad's suitcase. No big deal, I think to myself. I'll just push my way back to the top and go lounge on the sofa to watch the game. Part of me wonders why Dad laid his suitcase on top of the washing machine. It's vibrating up and down in a slow, steady rhythm.

As my head reaches the top of the suitcase, I push up with no luck. Someone closed it! I'm about to start meowing so someone will let me out, when I see something alarming. The zipper isn't closed completely, so I can finally see where the suitcase is.

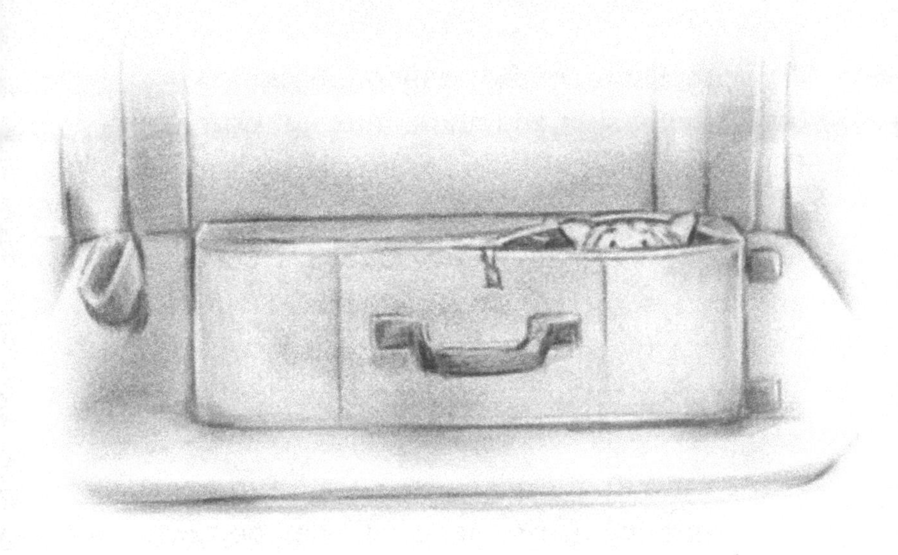

THE BACK OF DAD'S CAR!

How in the world did this happen? I must have been in a really deep sleep. Maybe we aren't far from home, and I can get Dad's attention so he can take me back there. I wiggle my head a little further out of the suitcase and look around. Oh no! I think to myself as I peer out past the zipper. I can see water in the distance through the car window. It looks like we are really high up in the air. The boats look tiny, and suddenly I get a frightening thought: We're on that really high bridge I've heard the girls talk about! Rosie says that every time they go on vacation in Ocean City, she closes her eyes tightly as they drive over the super scary bridge. Now I'm on that very same bridge! She wasn't kidding—it's terrifying!

With a soft cry, I quickly dig back down to my sleeping spot and start thinking. Come on Riley, what would Jack do? Jack is my brother cat who lives at home with me. He is older and wiser, doesn't get into any trouble, sleeps a lot, and always makes good decisions. He would know exactly what to do right now.

He'd curl up and go to sleep, I decide. There's nothing else TO do, unless I want to jump out of the car onto this giant bridge and run home. That certainly doesn't sound like a good idea. Nope, I will do what cats do best. I'll go back to sleep. Satisfied with my decision, I settle back into the clothes, listening to the sounds of the baseball game as I slowly drift back to sleep.

"Trey Mancini takes a step, swings, and connects! The ball flies deep into center field. It's over the wall! Home run Orioles!"

Chapter 3
Surprise!

Thump! Startled, I open my eyes and look around. I'm rolling sideways! I peek through the zipper and discover that Dad is wheeling his suitcase through the lobby of a hotel. We must have arrived in Ocean City for Dad's business trip.

"Welcome to Dunes Manor, Mr. Westnick. Your room is number 1021. Enjoy your stay with us."

I hear Dad say thanks, and then I'm rolling again, through the lobby, down a hallway, and into an elevator. Whoa! This feels like one of those amusement rides the girls always talk about. My stomach bounces around as the elevator stops, and before I know it, Dad's laying the suitcase down and unzipping it.

“What in the world?! Riley! How did YOU get in here?” Dad looks startled as he opens his suitcase and finds me. I look up at him with scared blue eyes. I try to tell him what happened, but it just comes out as a soft “Meow.”

“All you can say for yourself is ‘Meow,’ huh Riley,” Dad says. He smiles as he scratches my head. I purr instantly because he knows that’s my favorite place to be petted. “What am I going to do with you, buddy?”

I jump out of the suitcase and rub myself in a figure 8 between Dad's legs. He laughs and says, "I guess you'll have to make yourself at home. We're only here overnight. I'll go to the store and buy a litter box and some cat food for you."

Cat food! My tummy rumbles at those words. I hope he gets some good treats too. I jump up on the King-sized bed and get comfy while Dad goes out to buy me dinner. It seems like no time has gone by when I hear the door creak open and the sound of cat food plopping into the new dish.

"Only the best for my Riley," Dad says. I give him a quick purr, smack my tail on his leg, and devour my dinner. I am starving! That road trip made me really hungry. Dad unpacks his suitcase and we spend the rest of the night snuggled together watching ESPN. A cat sure could get used to this.

Chapter 4
Lazy day? No way!

The next morning starts out just like it would at home. I gobble up my breakfast and then lounge on the bed while Dad gets ready for work. As he straightens his tie, I hold myself back from lunging for it. I learned once before that a tie is not a toy, after I tried to grab it off Dad's neck one day. He wasn't happy with the scratch I left on his belly.

"All right, Riley," Dad says as he puts on his jacket and picks up his briefcase. "I have meetings all day today, so just hang out and don't get into any trouble. I'll leave the balcony door open so you can get some fresh air. Go find a nice place to sleep."

After Dad leaves the hotel room, I saunter out to the balcony. It's a beautiful day, with clear skies, and the sun is shining brightly. I find a warm spot to lie in the sun and stare out at the ocean. What a calm day this is going to be, I think to myself. I have barely closed my eyes when all of a sudden I hear a squeaky voice right next to me.

"Hello there, kitty!"

I jump and howl! Startled, I see a funny looking bird standing on the ledge of the balcony staring at me. He is mostly white with grey feathers and a small, yellow beak. Back at home, I love watching the birds fly around in our backyard. Mom always tells me I can't go out and chase them, after I tried to go through the glass door once. That hurt my head for a long time! This guy looks friendly and different from all of those birds I've seen.

"What, or rather, who are you?" I ask this strange creature.

"I'm Bagel and I'm a seagull. I've never seen you around here before. Are you on vacation?"

Bagel seems friendly, so I relax and answer, "Kind of. I fell asleep in my owner's suitcase and ended up here. I'm Riley and I'm a cat. How did you get the name Bagel?" I ask curiously.

"Funny you should ask. There's a joke I've heard people tell when they're here on the boardwalk. See if you can figure it out. Why do seagulls fly over the ocean?"

I think for a minute but have no idea. He says, "Because if they flew over the bay, they would be bay-gulls!" We both laugh hysterically, and I know in that instant we will be good friends.

"Are you going to lie here all day?" Bagel asks me as he walks around the balcony.

"I'm supposed to stay out of trouble," I respond as I stretch out my long limbs on the chair.

"I can keep you out of trouble, but still show you all the sights downy ocean, hon!" Bagel says with a Baltimore accent.

I laugh. He sounds just like those commercials I've heard about Ocean City. "Sounds good, Bagel. Where do we start?"

"Well, first we have to get you down from here. It's easy for me since I can fly, but you're a little tougher. Hmm…" says Bagel as he looks around for a way to escape.

Before he can say another word, I jump off the balcony.

Chapter 5
Boardwalk With Bagel

"RILEY!!" Bagel yells as he flies over the ledge, expecting to see me splattered like a pancake on the boardwalk below.

"I'm right here, Bagel," I respond calmly, casually walking down the wall. "I do this all the time at home," I say as I put one paw in front of the other.

"Whoa, Riley!! You're going to fall! Cats can't walk down buildings. They climb up things and then get stuck. It's what they're known for," Bagel rushes to try to stop me. His eyes get wide as he watches me continue my trek down the wall. "No way! That's quite a super power, Ri!" Bagel says as he flies down the wall next to me.

"I didn't know it was special," I say as I make my way swiftly down the wall. Jumping to the bottom, I look back at Bagel, who still stares at me in disbelief. "I thought all cats could do it. I mean, Jack sleeps all the time, but I still figured he could climb down a wall if he wanted to. Can't he?" I ask. I am nervous, hoping my new friend won't think I am a strange cat.

"Probably not, dude. I've never seen a cat do that," Bagel says. I am relieved. He seems impressed rather than weirded out. He continues, "All right, now that we're safely on the ground, our adventure can start. Are you hungry, buddy? It's about time you have the best french fries on the planet—Thrasher's!"

Bagel leads me down the boardwalk. There are so many sights to see; I don't know where to look! We pass stores with colorful neon signs in the windows, an arcade with flashing lights and loud, booming music, games with darts and water balloons, and so many people! Some are in bathing suits headed toward the beach, and others are walking around enjoying the beautiful day. Finally, Bagel comes to a halt.

"Here we are," Bagel announces as he stops to gobble up a french fry off the ground. "Crazy humans, always letting these drop out of their buckets," Bagel says as he continues eating. "Come on, Riley. Get a load of this!"

I sniff the french fry, bat it with my paw a few times, and then take a bite. "Wow, Bagel! You weren't kidding. These are delicious! I wish they made french fry flavored cat food."

"These are Ocean City's finest french fries. They've been around a lot longer than I have, but are still as amazing as ever. Get a taste and then let's go down to Trimper's. We can play games and ride the best rides in town!"

Bagel and I continue walking down the boardwalk, stopping now and then to snag another fry. Nobody seems to notice the two of us. I guess people don't think it is odd for a cat and seagull to be hanging out together.

"Come on in here, Riley, but step carefully. You don't want to...Riley! No!"

I hear Bagel yell, but it doesn't matter. I have blocked out all sounds in my pursuit of the cat in front of me. I crouch down, shake my tail, and pounce.

That is the last thing I remember before everything goes black.

Chapter 6
Why go slow when you can go FAST

"Here you go, buddy. Come back to me. Smell the french fry."

Carefully, I open my eyes. Bagel is waving a fry back and forth under my nose.

"What happened, Bagel?" I ask in a daze as he drops the fry into my mouth.

"Welcome back, Riley. I thought we lost ya! I was trying to take you into the House of Mirrors, but you must have thought you saw another cat. Look around—it's all you!" Bagel explains.

I slowly turn my head this way and that. Everywhere I look, I see the same cat...me! Feeling silly, I get up, shake my back, and smile sheepishly at Bagel.

"No worries, Riley," he says. "Birds fly into glass doors all the time, remember? It happens to the best of us."

"Thanks, Bagel," I say, happy to have found such a good friend in this new town.

Together, we walk through the mirrors. We look so funny! Sometimes we are short and pudgy, and other times we look tall and skinny. As we exit, Bagel asks, "How do you feel about going fast?"

"Well, I've only ever gone fast in the car. Dad drives pretty slowly, but Mom likes to go faster. It's super fun! I meow a lot, and she always tells me it's ok. I wish I could tell her I love it," I say.

"Sweet! Let's check out some fun rides then!" Bagel exclaims.

We spend the morning going on one thrill ride after another. Bagel always finds a sneaky way for us to get onto each ride. We cram into the Wrecking Ball that whips us back and forth, up and down. Next comes the Merry Mixer. Around and around we spin! Feeling a little dizzy, we decide to take a break to go through the Funhouse. Bagel flies over the trick floors and the wobbly bridge, and my claws help me cross without any trouble.

"There's one more ride we have to go on. It's an Ocean City classic," Bagel says as we make our way toward the Tidal Wave.

As we climb into an empty seat, I ask, "What's so special about this roller coaster?"

"Just wait and see," Bagel tells me excitedly.

The ride starts, but instead of going forwards, we go backwards up, up, up a giant hill. When it reaches the top, it pauses for a moment and then we plummet down, speeding faster than even Mom does when she's driving!

"Oooh weeee!" Bagel and I yell.

The coaster loops around and I hang on with my claws for dear life! When we get back to the first hill, I am breathless.

"Great ride, Bagel!" I pant.

"Hang on, Riley! It's not over yet," Bagel laughs.

Without stopping, the roller coaster goes back up the hill. Slowly, we climb higher and higher. Suddenly there is a loud noise and then Whoosh! We fly backwards! The Tidal Wave speeds down, whips around the loop again, and then races back to where we began.

"What a rush!" I yell as we shakily make our way off the ride. "That was awesome!"

"I'm glad you liked it," Bagel says. I can tell he is relieved that I'm not about to throw up my french fry breakfast. "What do you say we check out more of Delmarva?"

"Del what a?" I ask.

Bagel laughs. "Delmarva. That's what the locals call this area. 'Del' is for Delaware, 'mar' is for Maryland, and 'va' is for Virginia. Ocean City is just one town along the Eastern Shore. There are so many more cool places we can see today. Let's go to Assateague Island."

Assateague? I decide not to ask him to explain what that is. Instead, I start to walk back up the boardwalk, but Bagel turns toward the water. "Um, Bagel? I know I can do some things other cats can't do, but swimming isn't one of them," I say nervously.

Bagel laughs. "Don't worry, Riley. I have a few friends who can help us out," he says as he walks toward the inlet. "Here's our ride."

I look around slowly. We are surrounded by all different sized boats. I look back at Bagel with a confused expression on my face.

"I spend a lot of time down here searching for fish," Bagel explains. "All the anglers know me. Those are fishermen," he explains when he sees that I am still confused. Then he continues, "Sometimes they let me perch on their boats when they go out to fish. I don't see why they wouldn't let you on board too."

"Searching for fish sounds like fun," I say, licking my lips.

Bagel laughs, "The french fries weren't enough for you, huh Riley? Let's hop on board a boat and see if we can get a ride and a snack."

Bagel leads me down the dock toward a small fishing boat. A tall man with a bright blue bucket hat is loading supplies onto the deck, while a shorter man with an Orioles cap is getting the boat ready to cruise. They don't look surprised when they see us.

"Hey there, Gully," the tall man says. "Are you looking for a ride? It's a beautiful day to be on the water. We're heading down to Assateague this morning if you want to join us."

I look at Bagel. “Gully?” I ask.

Bagel smiles. “That’s what they’ve named me. I can’t very well tell them my name is Bagel, now can I?”

I laugh and reply, “No, I guess you can’t.”

Just then, the shorter man notices me. “Who’s your friend, Gully?” he asks. “Does he want some fishies too?”

Knowing just what to do to win him over, I walk up, purr, rub myself against his legs, and stare up at him with my big blue eyes. Nobody can ever seem to refuse me when I do that.

"Aw, what a sweet kitty. Looks like you do want a boat ride today," he says as he runs his hand down my back. "Ok boys, hop up and let's go for a ride," he says.

Bagel flies to the railing and I climb aboard the small boat. The men untie the ropes and we set sail for Assateague Island. Bagel and I are quiet for most of the ride, and I try to take in all the new sights. Cats don't get to ride in boats very often! The wind against my face and the mist of water off the ocean feels cool in the hot sun. I curl up against the side of the boat and before long, fall into a deep sleep.

Chapter 7
A Pretty Penny

"Check it out, Riley!"

I awake to Bagel nudging me with his wing. Slowly opening my eyes, I look around. While I was sleeping, the boat had traveled south to a new place. "Welcome to Assateague Island," Bagel says. As I look around, I am in awe of the seemingly endless stretch of beach. Sunbathers are scattered here and there, soaking in the sun. I even see cars further down on the beach. I didn't know you could drive on sand! Out in the water, I watch as surfers try to catch the perfect wave. What an amazing place! I know Bagel is going to want to explore, but I have no idea how I am going to get off the boat and onto land.

As if reading my mind, the tall man says, "I can steer the boat a little closer to shore. Think you can jump onto the beach from here, kitty?" He slows the boat and pulls it as close to the shore as he can.

I climb onto the railing and look out at the water. Waves splash up against the side of the boat and rock it back and forth. I know I am good at jumping since I pounce on paper balls at home all the time, but this is frightening.

"You can do it, Riley. I know you can," Bagel says encouragingly.

Mustering up my courage, I meow goodbye to the anglers and leap off the boat. I soar through the air just like a bird! What an incredible feeling!

"Go, Riley, go!" Bagel yells as I fly over the waves. In no time at all, my feet touch the sand for the first time.

"Whoa! What is this stuff?" I ask, putting my nose to the ground.

Bagel laughs as I look up at him.

"What is it? Why are you laughing at me?" I ask.

"Shake yourself out, Ri. This is sand, and you have it all over your nose!" Bagel says through hysterics.

Slightly embarrassed, I shake myself out and try to use my paw to brush sand off my nose. As you can imagine, if you've ever been to a beach, all I do is put MORE sand on my nose! I can't help but laugh right along with my new friend. All of a sudden, I hear a new voice.

"Best way to clean sand off your nose is to dunk your face in water."

I look up and am frightened. Staring back at me is a huge animal, bigger than any cat I have ever seen before. Its body is chestnut brown, except for patches of white on its massive legs, tail, and mane. This new animal's hooves are planted right next to me and look like they could squash me with one step. I look at Bagel to see if we need to run from this strange creature, but he is smiling again.

"Hello there! I'm Bagel, and this is my friend, Riley. We just left Ocean City on a fishing boat and thought we'd explore the southern end of Delmarva. What's your name?" Bagel asks. He isn't scared at all, probably because he could just fly away if he thought he was in danger.

"What fun! My name is Penelope, but my friends call me Penny. I'm a pony," she says when she sees that I am still looking at her timidly. "I don't see many animals like you, Riley. Seagulls, yes, but what are you?" she asks.

Penny seems friendly, but I am still a little scared. "I'm a cat," I say, trying to look big and brave. "I traveled with my owner on a business trip, met Bagel, and ended up here."

Penny smiles. "You look like a big, brave cat," she says, making me feel less nervous. "How exciting! You picked the best day to visit. Today is the annual pony swim from Assateague to Chincoteague Island in Virginia. I was just heading there now to meet my friends. I can't think of a better way for you to see all the sights today, Riley. If you want, you can ride on me down the beach and across the water. I promise I will go slowly and be careful," she adds when she sees that I am still unsure.

Be brave, Riley, I say to myself. "Ok, Penny, if you're sure it's safe," I reply. Penny bends her two front legs and lowers her head to the ground. Here goes nothing, I think as I carefully climb up her mane and settle onto her back. She slowly raises herself up, and I look around to take in the sights.

"This is my home," Penny says as she starts walking down the beach. "I have lived here all my life. My family is waiting for me down by the water, along with a bunch of my friends. They've already been herded into the Corral," she says.

"What's the Corral?" Bagel asks, flying along next to us.

Penny explains, "It's the area where all of the horses wait before we can go across the water to get to Chincoteague."

"What happens then, Penny?" I ask.

"Well, we get to march down the street in a parade and then go to an auction. We will either get to go home with a new owner or come back here to Assateague. Either way, I'm excited. It's a new adventure for me, and I love adventures," Penny says, genuinely excited. She continues, "Hold on tightly, Riley. I need to gallop a little faster to be able to make it in time."

Before I have time to think about what gallop means, Penny takes off down the beach. I sink my claws into her mane and hold on as

she gallops through the sand toward a herd of ponies waiting by the water. As we approach the other horses, we hear a voice coming through a megaphone.

"Get ready, ponies! The swim is about to start!" a man announces loudly.

"Riley, you're going to need to climb up higher," Penny tells me. "Once I start swimming, most of my body will be under the water. Climb onto my head and you should stay pretty dry."

Trusting my new friend once again, I climb

atop her head just as the ponies begin swimming across the Assateague Channel. Penny joins in with the herd, and off we go.

"Mind if I join you?" Bagel asks right before he perches on top of MY head.

I peer up at Bagel. "I bet nobody has ever seen a seagull on a cat on a horse before!" I say laughing.

Penny laughs as she continues her swim across the water. All around us, ponies splash as they swim across the Channel. People on the shore and in boats cheer for us as we continue our journey. What an incredible ride! I can't believe that in such a short amount of time I have already done so much. I walked the boardwalk in Ocean City, rode rides at Trimpers, sailed on a fishing boat, and now this.

As if reading my mind, Bagel says, "This is just the beginning, Riley. I have so much more in store for you today."

Smiling, I hold on tightly as Penny finishes swimming and walks ashore on Chincoteague Island. She seems exhausted as she joins the other ponies who made the journey. Before long, we hear another loud announcement.

"Time for the Pony Parade!"

"Will you both stay with me for the parade?" Penny asks. "What a sight I will be if I have two extra friends riding on my head!"

"Absolutely, Penny. This is the most fun I've had in a long time!" I reply excitedly.

Penny holds her head high as she joins her friends in the parade. As she saunters down Main Street, I can hear voices all around, talking about us.

"Look at that pony, Mommy! Do you see what's on its head?" A little boy shouts as he points toward Bagel and me.

"Is that a cat?! And a seagull, too?! I've never seen anything like it!" someone else says incredulously.

I look up at Bagel and he smiles down at me. We feel like royalty as Penny marches us down the street. Onlookers take pictures, point, and cheer at us as we make our way to the carnival grounds.

Finally, Penny stops and says, "This is where my journey ends. I wait here with the other horses and then the auction will begin. That's when I'll find out where I'm going," she explains.

"Then this is where we leave you," Bagel announces as he flies off my head. I follow, climbing down off Penny's back. "I promised Riley we would explore all of Delmarva, and while this is a great start, I have so much more to show him. We've been to Maryland and Virginia, so it's about time we traveled to the 'Del' area of Delmarva," Bagel says with a grin.

"Thanks for the ride, Penny. Good luck in the auction," I say to my new friend.

"I'm so glad I found you guys," Penny says. "This was such a fun day, and I'll remember it forever. Maybe someday we'll meet up again."

"I hope so," I say as I rub myself in between Penny's legs, not scared anymore that she will step on me. In response, she nudges me gently with her muzzle, and then I walk away with Bagel.

"Time to head north, Riley," Bagel says as he walks along a path leading to the water. Up ahead at the end of the path, I see what look like the scooters that Nicki and Rosie like to ride around our neighborhood.

"Um, Bagel? How are we going to get up north?" I ask hesitantly.

"Trust me, Riley," Bagel replies with a mischievous smile.

Never trust a seagull.

Chapter 8
Jet Skis, Speed Boats & Dolphins

Bagel flies onto the handlebars of one of the big scooters and looks back at me. "Come on, Riley. You're about to learn how to drive a jet ski!"

Jet ski? I don't know what Bagel is talking about, but I have trusted him this far, and we haven't gotten into trouble yet. Cautiously, I climb onto the seat of the jet ski.

"There you go, Riley. Now it's time to have a little fun. I've seen people drive these all over the water. You're a special cat. I know you can do it," Bagel says, putting his trust in me. "Sit here like this, put your paws up here on the handles, push here, and off we go," Bagel demonstrates and makes it all sound really easy. He perches on my back and looks at me, waiting.

Taking a deep breath, I push my fear aside and do what Bagel had explained. The jet ski roars to life and shoots off away from the dock!

"Whoooeeee!!!" Bagel exclaims as he holds

onto my back. "Way to go, Riley!! Keep the sand on your left and just keep going!"

I can't believe it! I am driving a jet ski up the Atlantic Ocean. Me, a quiet little tabby cat from the suburbs of Baltimore! Riding in the fishing boat was fun, but this is unbelievable! The jet ski cuts a path through the water as I steer it north toward Ocean City. Every once in awhile, fish jump out of the water around us, and I wish I could snatch one for a treat. As we ride past a fishing boat, I see the passengers' jaws drop, not believing what they are seeing. Before long, the inlet is back in sight and we are getting closer to the dock.

"Let go of the throttle and we'll coast towards the dock," Bagel yells over the sound of the engine. Again, trusting my friend, I do what he said. We cruise into the inlet and then jump off the jet ski onto the dock. People stare at us incredulously as I run away from the water with Bagel on my back! All of a sudden, Bagel flies off and lands right in front of me.

"Welcome to the Sea Rocket!" he exclaims.

Bagel looks at me with so much excitement on his face that all I can do is laugh. "What is the Sea Rocket?" I ask.

"It's just the fastest, bumpiest boat in the sea!" Bagel exclaims. "There's no quicker way to cruise the ocean than the Sea Rocket, even by jet ski."

We stand in front of American flags, staring at a large boat. Tourists are already packed onto it, waiting for the ride of their lives. Bagel leads me toward the back of the boat. "Get your claws ready," he says.

As Bagel settles onto a post on the boat, I look around for a way to hold on. A life preserver ring catches my eye as the boat starts to pull away from the dock. I squeeze into it snugly just in the nick of time.

"Whoa!!!" I meow as the boat speeds away from the inlet. I am getting really good at riding fast rides. I am just happy I'm not driving this time. Bagel and I ride in silence as the wind whips our fur and feathers around. This is much different from the fishing boat we rode on earlier. We bump and bounce as the boat soars over the waves. I never expected my day to be this exciting.

"What do you think?" Bagel shouts over the roar of the engine.

"It's incredible!" I yell back.

"Glad you like my home," says a new, squeaky voice to my left. I look over and see a grey and white animal I have never seen before. It is jumping alongside the boat and diving back into the water.

"Who are you?" I ask.

"My name's Bo. I'm a bottle nosed dolphin. Who are you?" he asks.

"I'm Riley and this is my friend, Bagel," I reply. The whole time I talk, Bo keeps jumping.

"Nice to meet you! I see a lot of seagulls around here, but can't say I've ever seen a cat," Bo says.

By this time, most of the people on the boat are standing by the edge taking pictures of Bo. He entertains the crowd by jumping higher and making huge splashes in the water. I laugh and shake myself as his latest splash ends up on me.

“Where are you headed?” asks Bo.

“Riley here has never been to the Eastern Shore,” Bagel explains to Bo. “We explored the southern part of Delmarva this morning, and now I want to show him around the northern end.”

“I am heading that way myself,” Bo says as he does a flip in front of the boat. He is quite a performer. “Bagel, I know you can fly, but how is Riley going to get from the boat to the shore?”

"Huh, I hadn't thought about that," Bagel says, scratching his head with his wing. "I don't think I can carry him," he says, looking down at his webbed feet.

"Don't you worry guys," Bo says. "I have the perfect plan and a buddy who can help us out. Hop on my back, Riley, and I'll take you for a ride."

Without questioning him, I jump on. Looking back, I see the surprised looks on the faces of the people on the boat. I guess they've never seen a cat ride a dolphin before. They are in for a treat!

Chapter 9
Riding the Waves

"Hang on tightly to my dorsal fin—don't worry, it won't hurt me a bit!" Bo yells.

I sink my claws into the pointy fin on top of Bo, and he takes off in front of the boat. Bagel flies alongside us, hooting with excitement.

Did I say before that the Sea Rocket was the best ride of the day? Well, that's because I hadn't yet ridden a dolphin! Bo keeps his fin out of the water so I won't get too wet and thrashes his tail back and forth to propel us forward. Before I know it, the Sea Rocket is out of sight, and we are swimming past sections of beach I haven't seen before. Along the coast I see big houses, huge condos, and tons of people sunbathing on the beach. In the water, swimmers jump over waves or ride boogie boards. A few boats are farther out toward the horizon.

"Where are we?" I ask Bo. He is slowing down as we approach a huge ferry boat.

"Welcome to Lewes, Delaware," Bo answers. "I love it up here because it's much less crowded than downtown Ocean City. Everyone on the Cape May-Lewes Ferry loves it when I jump around and do tricks."

Bo comes to a complete stop, but we are still far away from the shore. Bagel flies up next to us and looks as confused as I am feeling.

"Bo, this has been a great ride, but how in the world am I going to get to the beach?" I stare nervously at the waves crashing in front of me. A little water on my face is one thing, but submerging myself in the ocean is another story.

"I told you not to worry yourself, kitty friend. My sea buddy will help us. Here's Barny now!" Bo waves his tail at a diamond-shaped creature that is swimming toward us.

"Hey, Bo! Who are your friends?" the creature asks.

"This is Riley the cat and Bagel the seagull. Guys, this is Barny. He's a skate," Bo explains.

"My owners always talk about going outside to skate," I say. "Do they hang out with you, Barny?"

Barny and Bo laugh. "I'm not that kind of skate, Riley. You've never been to the ocean before, have you?" Barny asks. I shake my head. "I'm a kind of fish, but please don't eat me!"

I laugh. "Don't worry! I don't eat my friends," I tell him. I am excited to make another friend today.

"Barny, Bagel wants to take Riley into Lewes to see the sights. Think you could help get him to shore?" Bo asks.

"Of course! I was hoping to surf the waves today!" Barny exclaims.

"This is where I leave you then, friends," Bo says. "Come back and visit sometime, Riley."

"Thanks for the swim, Bo," I say as I climb onto Barny's outstretched back. "This was the most fun I've ever had."

Bo answers by flipping into the air and landing on his back with a splash. We all laugh and then Barny says, “Hold on tight!” I have heard those words a lot today already. I dig my claws in and prepare for another ride as Barny takes off for the shore.

Chapter 10
Beach Buddy

"Gnarly!!" Barny yells as he surfs on top of a giant wave. "Isn't this cool, Riley?"

Cool isn't the word to describe it. Out of this world is more like it! I can't believe something like this is happening to me, Riley, the little, well kind of fat, cat from Baltimore. I am on the back of a skate, surfing waves in the Atlantic Ocean.

I cling to Barny's back tightly as he sails into the shore, Bagel flying right next to us. When we get to the beach, I jump off into the sand, right onto something sharp and pointy.

"Ouch!" I jump to the side and look down towards the sand. Staring back at me is a little animal with a hard shell, two beady eyes, eight little legs, and two giant claws. I thought I had claws, but they are nothing compared to this thing.

"Who and what are you?" I ask hesitantly.

"My name is Cuddles. I'm a blue crab. I live here in the ocean but heard a commotion on the beach so I thought I'd check it out. Who and what are you? I've never seen anything like you before," Cuddles says. He looks a little scared, too, and still has his claws raised.

"I'm a cat. My name is Riley, and these are my new friends, Barny the skate and Bagel the seagull. We won't hurt you, if you don't plan to hurt us," I tell Cuddles.

He smiles and lowers his claws. "Sorry, Riley, I always have to be prepared to defend myself. You never know who might try to eat me. People around here seem to want to do that a lot," Cuddles says. "What is a cat doing on the beach?"

Bagel answers, "Nice to meet you, Cuddles. I

found Riley sleeping on a balcony in downtown Ocean City. I took him out for an adventure and here we are! We met a dolphin named Bo on our way up north and he introduced us to Barny here. These two just surfed into shore. I want to show Riley around town and thought I'd start with the lighthouse. Want to come with us?"

"I've never been to a lighthouse before!" Cuddles replies. "I spend most of my time alone down here on the beach, so I don't get to see much of anything else. I would love to come, but I don't want to slow you down. I don't move nearly as fast as the rest of you," he says sadly.

Without hesitation, I speak up. "Cuddles, you can ride on my back. So many friends have helped me out today. Let me help you this time. Just...keep those claws closed," I say cautiously.

Cuddles laughs. "Thanks a lot, Riley," he says. "You don't have to worry about me. I'll just use them to hold a little fur so I don't fall off." He climbs carefully onto my back and snuggles into my fur.

"I guess that's why they call you Cuddles," I laugh as the crab makes himself at home on my back.

The trio of us wave goodbye to Barny as he dives back out into the ocean. "Thanks for surfing with me, Riley!" Barny yells as he swims out into the sea.

Chapter 11
Hanging with the Gulls

"The sand can be hot, Riley. It's best to go quickly," Bagel warns.

"Thanks for the warning. Hold on tight, Cuddles. I'm a quick cat," I say to the crab on my back. All of my time playing with Nicki and Rosie has made me a fast runner. I take off across the sand, kicking up piles of it as I run.

Bagel wasn't kidding! The sand is scorching from the sunshine beating down on it all day. I dart quickly across it until I get to a patch of grass.

"This is the dune. It should feel a little cooler on your paws," says Cuddles from my back. "That was an incredible ride, Riley! I've never gone that fast before. It was so much fun!"

"Wow!" exclaims Bagel as he lands next to us. "I've never seen a cat move so quickly! First, you climb down a wall, and now you're speedy cat. What will we learn about you next?"

I laugh. "I really didn't know I could do anything special, Bagel. I'm just an ordinary cat."

"An EXTRAordinary cat," says Bagel as he wraps a wing around me in a hug. "My new friend could be a celebrity kitty! Just make sure you remember me when you're rich and famous."

"Sure thing, Bagel," I laugh. "Now, which way to the lighthouse?"

Bagel leads the way through the dunes, pointing out sights along the way. "We are in the middle of Cape Henlopen State Park," he tells us. "People come here all the time to walk along the trails and go on the beach. My favorite thing to do, though, is to sit at the top of the lighthouse. Come on, it's just over here."

Bagel detours from the dunes and heads toward the water. I am nervous that we'll have to take another ride somehow, but then I see where he is going. A path of rocks leads to a lighthouse that towers up into the sky.

"Riley," Bagel calls, "do you think you can climb up the lighthouse?"

"Sure, Bagel!" I call back. "Keep holding on tightly, Cuddles. First, you got to see me run quickly. Now you get to see me climb!"

Cuddles pinches my fur tighter as I begin my ascent up the lighthouse. "This is amazing!" he calls to me as I climb higher and higher, toward the sky and above the water.

"Look around and take it all in," Bagel says as I reach the top. "Over there, you can see the ferry, where we just were with Bo. That's the town of Lewes. If we kept going across the ocean, we would end up in Cape May, New Jersey," he continues. "The ferry goes back and forth every day from one town to the other."

"Have you ever been to Cape May?" Cuddles asks.

"Oh, sure I have. There's a great zoo there, and I have a lot of animal friends that I like to visit. I have flown all over, exploring new places. I always come back here, though. This is home," Bagel says.

"You better always come back! We would miss you," say voices I haven't heard before. Looking up, I watch as two seagulls fly to the top of the lighthouse and land next to us.

"Hi, Lily! Hey there, Ricky!" Bagel says, hitting wings with the birds. "Great to see you! Where have you been?"

"We spent the morning in Rehoboth Beach, trying to snatch french fries from people on the boardwalk," Lily says. "Who are your friends, Bagel?"

"This is Riley, and this is Cuddles. I'm spending the day showing Riley all around Delmarva, and we just met Cuddles along the way," Bagel says.

"Nice to meet you," I say to the seagulls. "How do you know Bagel?"

"This is our hangout," Ricky says. "All of the seagulls in the area like to explore, but we always meet up back here, at the top of this lighthouse."

"Where is Rehoboth Beach?" Cuddles asks.

Lily points down the coast. "If you keep traveling south along the water, you'll find Rehoboth Beach next. It has another beach, a long boardwalk, and TONS of french fries," she says.

"I'm taking them to Rehoboth next," Bagel tells his friends. "I just haven't decided how to get there. It's easy for us, since we're birds, but not as easy for a cat and a crab."

"The easiest way would be to follow the bike trail," says Ricky. "Maybe you could hop on the back of someone's bike or skateboard," he says to me.

"Skateboard?! I ride those all the time at home." My new friends look surprised, so I continue. "Rosie, one of my owners, loves to skateboard around her neighborhood. She thinks it's fun to put me on it and push me around. I've watched her enough times that I'm sure I could do it myself!"

"It's settled then. Let's go find a skateboard!" Bagel says, laughing.

"Have fun! Bagel, meet up with us later and tell us how the rest of your day went," Lily says as we start to make our way back down the lighthouse.

"Will do!" Bagel calls back to his bird friends. Then he turns to us and says, "All right, let's go find our ride, Riley."

Chapter 12
A Haunted Adventure

"Ready to roll?" Bagel asks.

We had walked to the bike trail and almost immediately found an abandoned skateboard. It was our lucky day! I got the hang of it after practicing for just a few minutes. Rosie would be so proud.

"I'm set if you are," I reply. "Cuddles, you know what to do."

"Hold on tightly!" he exclaims.

I kick off and, just like that, the three of us soar down the trail toward Rehoboth Beach. I can't believe how lucky I am that Bagel found me on the balcony this morning. Here I am now, riding a skateboard with a crab on my back! The sights from the top of the lighthouse were beautiful, but being down low like this has its own appeal. We ride across little bridges, through marshes, and next to the water. Every once in awhile, Bagel waves his wing at another bird flying by. He sure is popular! Before long, the trail meets up with a busy road, and we find ourselves surrounded by cars.

"This is Rehoboth Avenue," Bagel explains. "It's the main way into downtown Rehoboth Beach. We can follow it up to the boardwalk, and then see if we can find any treasures, like more fries."

"Sounds good, Bagel," I say as I push my skateboard along next to him. Stores and restaurants line the street as we make our way to the boardwalk. I stop to look in the window of a giant bookstore. "Nicki and Rosie like to read books to me," I tell my friends. "They line up all of their stuffed animals, and then I lie next to them while the girls read." Talking about Nicki and Rosie makes me miss them.

"That sounds really nice, Riley," Cuddles says as we continue walking. "I spend all of my time alone. I come onto the beach sometimes just to see what the people are doing, but most kids are scared, especially if they accidentally step on me in the water."

Bagel puts his wing around Cuddles. "It's a good thing you were on the beach today, Cuddles. Now you don't have to be alone all the time anymore. I can visit you anytime you want."

"Thanks, Bagel," Cuddles says smiling. "This is the most fun I've had in a long time."

"It's just beginning," Bagel replies. "Let's go see what we can find on the boardwalk."

When we arrive at the boardwalk, I park my skateboard by a bench so we can walk together. Bagel leads the way down the boards, stopping every so often to grab a fry that someone had dropped.

"These are amazing," Cuddles says as he nibbles on a french fry. "I've never crawled all the way up to the boardwalk before, and I've never found these on the beach. They're delicious!"

"Don't eat too much," Bagel says. "If we keep walking, we'll get to Funland, and you won't want to have full bellies for what we're going to do."

Bagel takes us down the boardwalk to an area full of rides, like the ones we rode on this morning. Lights flash and music plays as the rides spin in circles. Kids are playing games, too, trying to pound a frog onto a lilypad, or hit a mole with a hammer as it pops up. I look up at Cuddles on my back, and his eyes are wide. I'm sure he has never seen anything like this before.

"This is incredible!" Cuddles says. "Have you ever ridden on rides like these before?" he asks me.

"Bagel took me on rides similar to these this morning," I tell Cuddles. "These are a little different though. What do you want to ride, Bagel?"

"Everything!" he replies, and we all laugh. "We just have to be a little sneaky, so nobody notices us. Let's go see if we can find an empty tea cup."

Tea cup? I have seen my owner drink tea before, but I have no idea why a tea cup would be at an amusement park. Bagel leads us to the back corner, where giant, colorful tea cups are arranged in a circle. We scoot into an empty one, just as it starts slowly moving.

"You know the drill, boys," Bagel yells over the music. "Hold on!"

There is a round bar in the center that I hold

onto with my claws, as Cuddles tightly grips my fur. Round and around we spin, this way and that, faster and faster.

"Woohoo!!!" I hear Cuddles yell as the ride continues. I am relieved to hear he is having fun instead of being scared, or worse, sick!

"Let's go on more rides!" Cuddles says as the tea cups slow down. "That was amazing! I've never felt anything like that before. Lead the way, Bagel!"

"Sure thing, crab buddy," Bagel replies. He takes us onto the Sea Dragon, which looks like a big boat that rocks high in the sky from one side to another. My stomach hops all around as we go back and forth. Next, we climb onto the Paratrooper, which is kind of like a fast ferris wheel. The views we can see from the top are a lot like our view from the lighthouse.

"It's so cool that you get to see sights like these all the time, Bagel," I say while the ride is stopped at the top.

"You know, Riley, I fly around all the time and get to see so many things. I've never thought about the fact that other animals don't get to do that. I'm so glad that you and Cuddles get to experience this today," Bagel says.

"It's most definitely something I will never forget," Cuddles says. "What's happening now,

Bagel?" he asks with a frightened look on his face. The ride has started moving again, but this time we are going backwards, just like we had on the Tidal Wave this morning.

"Uh oh, I know what's happening. Backwards!!" I yell, as Cuddles hides his face in my fur. I don't think he lifts his head until the ride comes to a halt. Dizzily, we climb down.

"One more stop," Bagel says. "The most famous attraction at Funland."

We follow Bagel to the front of a Haunted Mansion. Every once in awhile, a skeleton pops out to talk to the crowd standing in line.

"I don't like the looks of this, Bagel," I say, being a bit of a scaredy cat. Fast, thrill rides are one thing. Scary, haunted rides are another.

For the third time today, all Bagel says is, "Trust me." We follow him onto a seat and ride into a dark house, while creepy music plays. The first time the lights flash, I throw my paws around Bagel. A ghost pops out at us, and he quickly puts his wing around Cuddles. By the end, we are all screaming at the scary parts of the mansion. When the ride is over, we quickly go to the TV outside, where it shows a picture taken from inside the mansion. There we are: a seagull, a cat, and a crab, wrapped around one another in terror.

"I can't wait for the owner of the ride to see that one," Bagel says, laughing, as our hearts begin to stop racing.

"This was so much fun, Bagel," I say as we walk away from the rides. "Where to next?" I ask as my stomach growls loudly.

Chapter 13 Race to the Finish

"Hungry again, Riley?" Bagel asks. "Let's keep heading south. I know just what you need to satisfy your tummy. Grotto pizza! We'll go to a different town for that, but how should we get there this time?" He scans the area for something to ride on and suddenly his eyes get wide.

I follow his gaze and see what he had zeroed in on. "What is that?" I ask, looking at something that looked like a jet ski with wheels.

"It's a scooter. If you can drive a jet ski, then you can definitely drive a scooter!" Bagel says excitedly. "Let's go!"

Hesitantly, I climb onto the scooter and examine it. It doesn't look much different from the jet ski. Bravely, I say, "Ok, let's do this!" as I start up the engine. I am a natural! Who knew I had all these talents? I make a mental note to tell Jack all about it, as I follow Bagel and steer toward the road.

"Stay to the side in the bike lane, away from the cars!" he yells, as we veer out onto the highway. I see a sign up ahead for Dewey Beach, and notice groups of people eating at restaurants or heading to the beach. We are certainly giving the tourists a show today. We cruise through the town and down the main highway. This is much different from driving in the ocean. Out there, all I had to worry about were fish and slow boats. Here on the road, cars whiz by us at high speeds, sometimes honking their horns! We zoom forward over a big bridge, although not as high as the scary one I had ridden over with my owner. From the top of the bridge, I can see water to my left and right.

"Where are we now, Bagel?" I yell to my seagull friend.

"This is the Indian River Inlet Bridge," he calls back to me. "On your left is the Atlantic Ocean, and on your right is the Indian River Bay. Look at all of those boats!"

I sneak a peek to the bay at my right and see fishing boats, motor boats, and jet skis. Some people have their boats docked at a sandbar and are in the water, throwing a football back and forth. Peering to the ocean on my left, I see waves crashing against rocks, and people playing on the beach. I turn my eyes back to the road in front of me as we go down a steep hill, and before long, I am parking the scooter next to what looks like a giant totem pole in Bethany Beach.

"This is Chief Little Owl. He watches over the town," Bagel explains as we look up towards the sky. "It's been here for years," he continues, "and it's the best way to know you've arrived in Bethany Beach."

"It doesn't look like an owl," Cuddles says curiously as he looks up.

"It represents the Nanticoke Indian Tribe," Bagel explains as he begins to lead us toward the boardwalk. "Years ago, they lived in this area, and many still do today."

Leaving Chief Little Owl behind us, we follow Bagel past more stores and restaurants, and even another bookstore. As we get closer to the boardwalk, I see tons of people gathering around. Music is playing, and most of the people look like my owner does before she goes outside for a run.

"What do you think is going on, Bagel?" I ask.

"Looks like a race is about to start," he replies.

"What's a race?" asks Cuddles.

"I know what a race is!" I exclaim. "One of my owners, Nicki, is a really fast runner. I've heard her talk about running in races before. She even won a medal once," I say proudly.

"People gather at the starting line," Bagel explains to Cuddles, who still looks confused. "Then, when the horn blows, they all start running. The first person to cross the finish line is the winner."

Suddenly, I have a crazy idea. "I'm going to run the race," I tell my friends.

"You? But you're a cat!" Cuddles says.

"Remember how quickly I ran across the hot sand, Cuddles? Bagel called me a speedy cat. I bet I can outrun all of these racers. Think about it," I continue when both of my friends still look at me skeptically. "When am I going to have this opportunity again? We have done so many unbelievable things today. What's one more?"

"I can't argue with that," Bagel says. "Cuddles and I will make our way to the finish line and wait for you there. Good luck, Riley!"

"I hope I can crawl there before you finish the race," Cuddles jokes.

As my friends walk away, I quickly move to the front of the pack of racers and wait by the starting line. A few people reach down to pet me, which feels so nice. They probably think I am just a stray cat who needs love. Just wait until they see me run!

"Runners, take your places!" I hear an announcer say through a megaphone. The crowd of racers pack together as they move even closer to the starting line. I crouch down, with my front paws stretched out in front and my backside up in the air. I am ready!

Suddenly, a loud horn sounds, and we are off! I sprint down the path, making sure none of the runners step on me. I feel more like a cheetah than a house cat. Feeling the wind on my face as I run reminds me of the boat ride we took this morning to Assateague Island. I can't help but think of all the remarkable things we've done today. Now here I am, running my very first race. If only Nicki could see me!

I round a curve and keep on running. I can hear spectators talking about me, but I block them out and stay focused on the race. Up ahead, I can see a few racers. I've never considered myself competitive, but I really want to beat them to the finish line. Slowly I start gaining on them, until it is just one other runner and me.

He is so focused on running that he doesn't see that there is a cat next to him! Ooh, I have a great idea, I think. I meow loudly and it works! The surprised runner looks down at me and slows his pace just enough that I overtake him. I can see the finish line up ahead! To the right of me is the ocean, and all around me, crowds of people are cheering.

"Let's go, kitty!"

"Run like a cheetah, little cat!"

"Almost there!"

With one final boost of energy, I sprint across the finish line. Bagel and Cuddles are waiting there for me, just as excited as the rest of the crowd.

"You did it, Riley!" Bagel exclaims as he throws his wing around me. "Did you hear everyone cheering for you? You really are a celebrity cat!"

"Thanks, Bagel! What a rush," I say. All around me, people are coming to see and pet the cat that had taken first place. It's not every day you see a cat running a race in Bethany Beach.

"We'd like to invite our winners to come up and receive their medals," an announcer says from the stage. "It's been quite an incredible day. We had more racers than ever before, including a very special racer who happened to come in first place. If Speedy Cat is still here, I would love to present him with a medal."

Speedy Cat! That's me! I wind my way through the crowd and onto the stage. After rubbing myself in between the announcer's legs, I sit down at his feet and stare out into the crowd. This is an amazing feeling!

"We didn't have any cat-sized medals," the announcer says, as everyone laughs, "but our friends at the local pet store quickly made a tag for our special winner here. It reads '1st place, Speedy Cat.' Kitty, I hope we see you again here in Bethany," he says, as he attaches the tag to my collar.

Reading my original tag, the man says, "Let's hear it once more for Riley, our Speedy Cat!" I meow loudly in appreciation, and everyone claps and cheers.

"All of this running and attention has made me hungry," I tell my friends as I rejoin them on the boardwalk after the medal ceremony.

"I bet it has. Follow me and I'll take you to the most delicious pizza in town," Bagel says.

Cuddles climbs up onto my back again as Bagel leads us to a restaurant with the most mouth-watering scent I have ever smelled. I close my eyes and breathe in the aroma.

"If we go around back, I'll find us some leftovers in the dumpster," Bagel says. Before long, he has found us breadsticks, slices of pizza, and more french fries!

"Mmmm," Cuddles says as he nibbles on a breadstick. "I've never had anything like this before."

"My owners get pizza at home sometimes, but I've never snagged a bite. It doesn't smell as good as this though," I say, as I chew my way through a slice of pizza.

"Don't get too full," Bagel says, with a mouth full of french fries. "I have a few more places to show you, and they all involve eating. Cats like fish, right?"

"We sure do," I reply, licking pizza sauce off my lips. "How are we going to get to the next place?"

"Well, how tired are your legs?" Bagel asks. "The next town isn't too far away. Think you could manage another run?"

Eating had brought my energy back, and I'm not sure I am up for driving another scooter. "Sure," I reply. "Climb aboard, Cuddles!"

Cuddles resumes his position on my back, and the three of us set off for another adventure.

Chapter 14
Here, Fishy Fishy

"Welcome to Fenwick Island!" Bagel announces as we make our way into the next southern town.

"This doesn't look like an island," Cuddles says, surveying the area.

"Well, it's not an island in the typical sense of the word," Bagel tells us. "It's more of a peninsula, but it's like a barrier island. There's not much separating the land from the water," he explains.

"It seems peaceful here," I say, enjoying the quiet. I am glad there aren't swarms of people around, like there were in the race in Bethany Beach.

"It usually is," Bagel says. "I like to come here to get away from all the noise. Plus, it has sushi!"

"What's shoe she?" Cuddles asks.

"Sushi? I know what that is. Every time my owners bring it home, I jump up on the table, hoping they'll feed me some, but they never do," I say sadly.

"Sushi is another yummy treat," Bagel

explains to Cuddles. "It has rice wrapped around any type of delicious seafood, vegetables, you name it."

"Seafood? Like crab?!" Cuddles asks, horrified.

"We'll stay away from eating crab," Bagel says reassuringly. "Follow me!"

Bagel leads us to the back of yet another restaurant with the most delicious smells. "One of the waiters brings me leftovers when I visit. He seems to like seagulls, so I'm sure he'll love you guys also." He perches on the window ledge and peers inside. Sure enough, after a few minutes, a man walks out with a tray.

"Great to see ya, seagull pal," he says, placing a tray of sushi on the ground for us. "Looks like you've made some friends too. Can't say I've ever seen a crab eat sushi before. Don't worry little guy, there's no crab in these rolls," he says to Cuddles.

I meow and rub myself between his legs. It's the only thing I can do to say thank you. The waiter scratches behind my ears and then leaves us to enjoy our feast.

"You've made some pretty incredible friends," I say to Bagel as I eat tuna out of one of the rolls.

"Flying around alone all day would be

boring," he says. "I've been lucky to find people who like animals. Sometimes they just need to talk to someone, and I guess since I can't really talk back, they find it easy to talk to me. I've heard all kinds of stories: one who wants to quit his job so he can travel, another who wants to go on a date with a pretty girl, but he's too nervous to ask her out, a little boy who was scared of the waves in the ocean, so I stood by him while he jumped at the shore line. I could go on and on," he says.

"Wow, Bagel. I sure am glad we get to be part of your story now," Cuddles says, nibbling on a piece of avocado.

"Me too, Cuddles. I'd take spending time with you two over flying around alone any time!" Bagel replies. "Now, who's ready for dessert?"

I laugh. "Bagel, you've treated us to some incredible meals today. I don't have much room left, but I trust that you know the best place for a snack."

"Oh, I sure do, buddy. It's time to head back to Ocean City. We're close to the Delaware/ Maryland state line, which is where we'll find the best popcorn."

"Lead the way!" Cuddles and I say, as we walk alongside our seagull friend.

Chapter 15
Popping in for Popcorn

"Mmmm, Fisher's popcorn," Bagel says as we cross the street.

"Is Fisher's popcorn made out of fish?" I ask, licking my lips. "More juicy fish sounds pretty tasty right about now."

Bagel laughs. "Sorry, Riley, but no. It's just the best popcorn around," he explains.

Bagel directs us to the parking lot of Fisher's. "People drop popcorn almost as often as they drop french fries," Bagel says. "We just have to look around."

Easily, my friends and I find popcorn pieces scattered everywhere: in the parking lot, on the grass, and by the trash cans. Cuddles climbs down to scrounge around for himself, and we have a popcorn feast together.

"Don't get too full, Riley," Bagel says. "We have one more stop left on this taste-testing tour before we have to head back downtown."

"Sounds good to me, Bagel," I say.

"This is where I leave you," Cuddles says

quietly. “The sun is getting lower in the sky, so I need to get back to my home. It’s time for me to go back into the water.” He scuttles over to Bagel and me and holds up his claw.

“It was great to meet you,” I say as I hit my paw against Cuddles’ claw. “Say hi to Bo and Barny for me if you see them again in the ocean.”

“Thanks for carrying me around on your back all day,” Cuddles says. “I had the time of my life! I never would have been able to go to the top of a lighthouse if it wasn’t for you. I’ll never forget this day.”

"Neither will I, Cuddles. It was the day I became friends with the coolest crab around," I say.

Bagel high-fives Cuddles' claw with his wing. "I'll come back and visit you too, Cuddles. This isn't the last you've seen of me. I have a feeling we are going to have many more adventures together, little buddy. Be sure to tell the other crabs in the ocean all about your day. You're going to be quite a popular crustacean from now on. Be careful getting back!"

"Don't worry about me. I'm hard headed," Cuddles jokes.

As he skitters away, Bagel turns back to me. "Let's go, Riley. Just a little time left now for the best ice cream in town. Just wait until you taste the Old Bay on it!"

Old Bay? Puzzled, I follow Bagel down the busy street until we arrive at a place every cat has dreamed about.

Chapter 16
A Cat's Dream Store

"King Kone. Home of King, the Gorilla, and some of the best, milkiest ice cream around," Bagel explains when we arrive.

I am barely listening. My jaw had dropped as soon as I saw the buckets of ice cream inside the window. My own palace full of milk! "How will we get some, Bagel? I can't imagine too many people drop goodies like this."

"This is the best part, Riley. I know the owner always gives his ice cream to dogs. Why not cats?" says Bagel. "Next time the door opens, scoot inside, meow, and purr really sweetly. See what happens."

I am not too sure that is a good idea, but the smell of ice cream lures me in. I wait for the last customer to walk out, and then dart into the store. Inside, I instantly find a sweet little girl who looks to be the same age as my Nicki. I go right up to her, purr, and rub against her legs.

"Oh, Daddy, look! This sweet cat just ran inside. I bet you want some yummy ice cream. Don't you, kitty kitty?" The girl scratches my head just how I love it. I purr and give a little meow.

"What's that, Lisa? Did you say something about a cat outside?" Her dad asks from behind the counter. He is busy cleaning up from the last set of customers. I meow again, and he finally notices me.

"Oh wow, a cat huh? You think you can just stroll in here and get a scoop of ice cream, do you, kitty?" he asks, coming around the counter to check me out. That, in fact, was exactly what I was hoping would happen. I leave the girl and walk over to the man, rubbing my tail against his leg. He smiles and reaches down to pet my back. I roll over and look up at him, purring.

"A cat that rolls over? Are you part dog?" he asks me, laughing again. "I can't turn away a customer, especially one as friendly as you," he tells me, as he walks back behind the counter. "At King Kone, we make sure everyone's happy. Lisa, take him outside and I'll bring out a bowl. What should I get you, kitty? Cotton Candy? Butter Pecan? Cookie Dough?"

All three please, I want to tell him, as the little girl scoops me up. I snuggle into her arms while she carries me outside. We sit on a bench together, waiting for my treat. I look around for Bagel, but he must be scrounging for food around the back of the store.

"Here you go, kitty," the man says, placing a bowl of ice cream on the ground for me. "Just plain vanilla for pets, but I sprinkled a little bit of Old Bay on top so you could have true Eastern Shore ice cream."

I leap down from Lisa's lap, ready to devour my meal. As I get closer, I see little bits of brown all over the top. What did this man do to my ice cream?! Cautiously, I sniff it and sneeze instantly. Lisa and the man laugh and watch while I decide to try again. This time, I lick the top instead. Wow! He was right! Somehow, the mix of spicy and milky sweetness is pure heaven. I close my eyes, lick, and purr.

"He loves it, Daddy!" I hear Lisa exclaim.

"Everyone does, girlfriend, apparently even cats," the man tells her as they go back inside the store to help another customer.

I lap up the ice cream and lick my lips in appreciation. I can't believe how amazing this day has been. From behind me, I hear a squawk and see Bagel there waiting for me. "Time to go, Riley. We need to get you back to the hotel."

"How are we traveling this time, Bagel? I've ridden on two boats, a dolphin, and a skate. I've carried a crab on my back while running. I've driven a jet ski and a scooter. What now?" I ask smiling.

"This time, my friend, we're going to do what all of the tourists do."

Chapter 17
Rooftop Promises

"This is what the tourists do?" I ask as we cruise down Coastal Highway on the top of a bus. Bagel had led me to the nearest bus stop, and while I climbed up the back of the bus, he flew to the top.

"Well, most of them ride inside," Bagel jokes. "I've never seen anyone ride on top before."

I laugh and say, "Bagel, this has been such a fun day. Thank you for showing me all around. I never expected when I woke up in that suitcase that I would end up riding down the highway on top of a bus!"

"I didn't know I would make such cool friends," Bagel replies smiling. "Our day isn't over quite yet. I have one more surprise for you, since you're such a talented cat."

I have no idea what Bagel means, but I have loved every one of his ideas today, so I have no doubt I will love this one. We ride in silence, taking in all of the passing sights. Before I know it, we are back at the hotel. We jump off at the closest bus stop and walk together toward the back.

"Follow me!" calls Bagel as he starts to fly up the building.

Thinking we are just going back to my balcony, I start climbing up, a little disappointed that our time together is over, but Bagel doesn't stop at my floor.

"Hey, Bagel! That was my balcony!" I call up to him.

"I told you. Our day isn't over yet!" he calls down to me as he keeps flying.

Smiling to myself, I continue to climb all the way to the roof of the Dunes Manor hotel. I find Bagel perched on the ledge, staring straight ahead. I make my way over to him, turn around, and am mesmerized.

"What do you think, Riley?" Bagel asks as I stare wide-eyed at the view before me. From the roof, we can just about see all of Delmarva, even more than we could see from the lighthouse in Lewes. Everywhere I look, I see colors and lights. Staring straight ahead, the massive expanse of water stretches out in front of me, with the spotlights of boats shining here and there. The people down below look like tiny ants from this height.

"Bagel, this is incredible," I breathe. "Everything is so beautiful."

"It's my favorite way to see the world," he replies. "Seagulls get to see it this way all the time, but cats usually don't. I'm glad I could show it to you, Riley. I spend most of my time flying around by myself, seeing all kinds of things. Today it was really fun to share these experiences with new friends."

"Most things are more fun when shared with friends," I say, smiling back at Bagel. "Can you imagine how boring it would have been if I had slept on that balcony all day? Look at all

I would have missed! Riding rides, trying new foods, meeting Bo, Barny, Penny, Lily, Ricky, Cuddles, and especially you, Bagel. Thanks for everything today."

We sit quietly together on the roof a little while longer. I try to make pictures in my head of everything I saw so I can really explain it all to Jack when I get home. He'll never believe the adventures I had today. Finally, I know it is time to go back to the balcony. Bagel flies down and perches on the railing while I climb down the side of the hotel.

"This is where I leave you, buddy," Bagel says sadly. "Just promise me one thing."

"What's that, Bagel?"

"Do this again. Climb into your owner's suitcase and travel the world. Get out of your house and see things. Think about everything you did today. All of our adventures. Don't you want to do that again? I know there are animals all over the world who would love to be your tour guide, like I was today. Find them and explore! Life is too short to sit around and nap all day."

Bagel is right. I love my home, my owners, and even Jack, but I was born to explore. Plus, I am good at it. I have talents that other cats don't have. I make up my mind.

"I promise, Bagel. I will find a way to get back here to see you someday too. Everywhere I go, I'll be sure to find a strong bird to send a message back to you, to let you know where I've been. Thanks for being such a good friend."

Bagel wraps his wing around me for a quick hug before flying off over the ocean. He really does get to see some amazing sights, I think to myself as I curl up on the balcony. It has been such a long day, and I am exhausted. I drift off to sleep, thinking about my promise to Bagel.

Chapter 18
If He Only Knew

"Where's my Riley?"

I hear the door slam and someone calling my name. Sleepily, I open my eyes and see my owner coming through the door. Even after all the fun I had today, I really did miss him. I run over meowing while he loosens his tie and kicks off his shoes. Looks like he also had a long, busy day.

Dad drops some cat food into my bowl for dinner. I wish I could tell him how full my belly is! I eat some of it to make him happy and then rub myself on his legs. It's really great to see him again. He scoops me up and snuggles on the bed with me while he turns the TV on to an Orioles game. "What a boring day you must have had, Riley. Locked up here with nothing to do but watch the birds."

If he only knew, I think to myself. I didn't just watch the birds, I flew with them! Unfortunately, all I can do is meow and purr at him. He scratches my ears in that place he knows I love. We lie on the bed together like that for the rest of the night. Even though I had such an incredible day, this is really nice. I guess he thinks so too, because what he says next echoes how I feel.

"This is really nice, Riley. I usually go to these meetings and then come back to a lonely, empty hotel room. Instead, tonight I get to cuddle here with you."

Aw, that makes me think of Cuddles, my crabby friend. I meow back at Dad.

"You like it too, huh? Well, maybe we can do this again. You didn't get into any trouble today, right?" Dad asks. I meow again. Boy, do I wish I could just talk. It would be so much easier! "Good boy. Looks like maybe you weren't meant to just sit around at home. I go away for another business trip next week. I might just have to pack you in my suitcase again," Dad says.

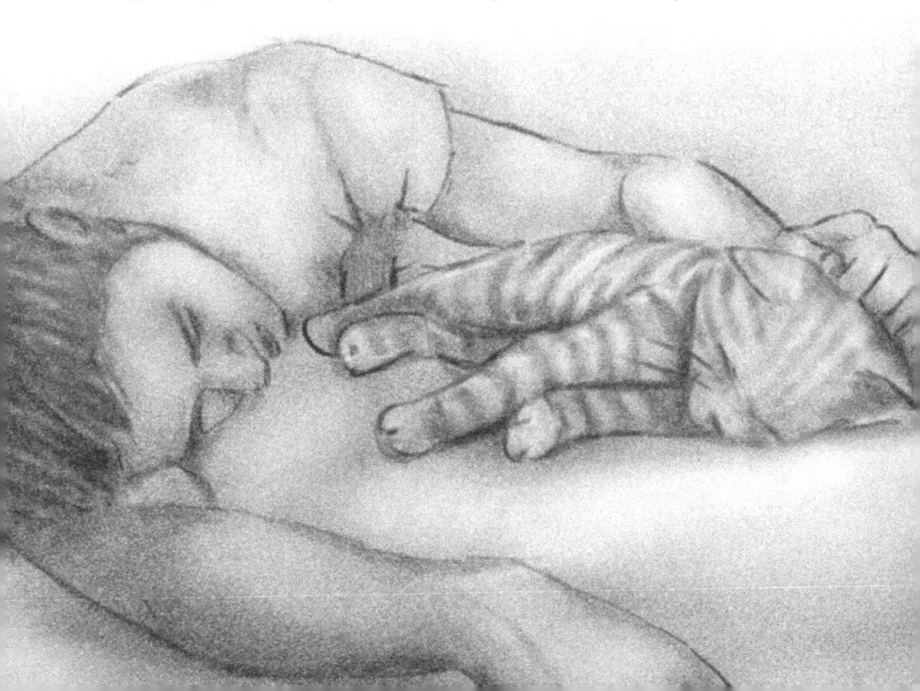

I can barely contain my excitement! Just like that, I am going to be able to keep my promise to Bagel. As Dad and I drift off to sleep, I have only one question going through my head.

Where will my next adventure be?

About the Author

Allison Wiest was an elementary school teacher for 12 years, but has had a passion for writing since she was young. In 2018, she left her teaching position to finally write the story that had been developing in her head for over five years. *Roaming Riley: A Delmarva Adventure* is Allison's first novel in what will be a series of books about Riley's adventures around the world. As a child, Allison spent one week every summer vacationing in Ocean City, Maryland with her sisters, parents, and grandparents. When she grew older, her family decided to move the vacation to Rehoboth Beach, Delaware. It seemed fitting that Riley's first adventure would be on the Eastern Shore, at the beach. Allison currently lives only 3 miles away from Ocean City in Selbyville, Delaware with her husband, two daughters, three cats, and a dog.

www.allisonwiest.com